Rabbids Invasion

Case File #7: Red Carpet Rabbids

by David Lewman

illustrated by Shane L. Johnson

Simon Spotlight

New York   London   Toronto   Sydney   New Delhi

Based on the TV series Rabbids® Invasion as seen on Nickelodeon™

SIMON SPOTLIGHT
An imprint of Simon & Schuster Children's Publishing Division
1230 Avenue of the Americas, New York, New York 10020
This Simon Spotlight hardcover edition March 2016
© 2016 Ubisoft Entertainment. All rights reserved. Rabbids, Ubisoft, and the Ubisoft logo are trademarks of Ubisoft Entertainment in the U.S. and/or other countries. All rights reserved, including the right of reproduction in whole or in part in any form. SIMON SPOTLIGHT and colophon are registered trademarks of Simon & Schuster, Inc. For information about special discounts for bulk purchases, please contact Simon & Schuster Special Sales at 1-866-506-1949 or business@simonandschuster.com.
Designed by Nicholas Sciacca
Manufactured in the United States of America 0116 FFG
10 9 8 7 6 5 4 3 2 1
ISBN 978-1-4814-5253-3 (hc)
ISBN 978-1-4814-5252-6 (pbk)
ISBN 978-1-4814-5254-0 (eBook)

CHAPTER 1:

Plunge In!

On a beautiful day, three Rabbids—those mysterious visitors from who knows where—ran through a big city, laughing. "BWAH HA HA HA!"

Even though it was a beautiful day, the Rabbids weren't at the park. They weren't at the zoo. They weren't at the beach.

Those all would have been excellent places to explore on a beautiful day.

But for some reason no one knew (including

the Rabbids themselves), the three invaders were running through a part of the city filled with factories. They dashed by huge brick buildings where people were making all kinds of things—blenders, toilets, toilet paper, those clips you put on bags of potato chips so they don't go stale . . .

Suddenly the Rabbid in front stopped.

He spotted something very interesting.

On a loading dock behind one of the factories, two big guys were loading crates onto a truck. One of the guys, Frank, had just finished his lunch, and his hands were greasy from eating potato chips. A crate slipped out of his hands. *CRASH!*

"Oops," Frank said, not really caring that he'd dropped a crate. He was thinking about looking for a more interesting job. Maybe president of the United States. Or possibly a fireman.

The crate broke open when it hit the ground, and everything inside spilled out.

That was what grabbed the Rabbid's attention.

Because what spilled out of the broken crate was a whole bunch of . . . *toilet plungers*!

Rabbids *love* toilet plungers!

"BWAH BWAH BWAH BWAH!" the Rabbid shouted, delighted. He ran over to the toilet plungers and started picking up as many of them as his stubby arms could carry.

When his two fellow Rabbids saw what he was doing, they both cried out, "BWAH BWAH BWAH BWAH!!!" They ran over and started gathering toilet plungers too.

"Hey!" Frank yelled. "Put those down!"

"Come on, Frank," the other guy (his name was Lamar) snarled. "Let's get 'em!"

The two big guys headed straight for the three Rabbids. When the Rabbids saw the two humans coming toward them, they laughed. "BWAH HA!" Then they started throwing toilet plungers at Frank and Lamar like spears.

Thwunk! One of the toilet plungers hit Frank right on the forehead and stuck there, like a wooden unicorn's horn.

The Rabbids pointed and laughed, rolling on the ground. "BWAH HA HA HO HO BWEEH HEEE!"

"HEY!" Frank shouted. "I DON'T APPRECIATE THAT!" He struggled to yank the toilet plunger off his forehead. Lamar grabbed on to the handle of the plunger to help him. *THHHHWOP!* The plunger came off, but both guys fell to the ground. Frank had a big red circle on his forehead.

That made the Rabbids laugh even harder.

Now Frank and Lamar were really mad. They ran straight at the Rabbids, growling in fury. "GRRRRRR!"

The Rabbids threw every toilet plunger they could get their hands on. But Frank and Lamar dodged the plungers or knocked them to the ground. Soon the Rabbids had run out of toilet plungers.

So they turned and ran.

But they didn't run away from the toilet plunger factory. They jumped onto the loading dock and ran through the big open doors, straight into the building.

"Bwhoaaaa," they said, amazed and delighted by what they saw.

Toilet plungers. Toilet plungers everywhere! Toilet plungers being made! Toilet plungers being tested! Toilet plungers being put in crates! Thousands of toilet plungers!!!

Within seconds the Rabbids had made their way into the huge mazelike factory, leaving Frank and Lamar behind.

"Where'd they go?" Frank said.

"Ah, who cares?" Lamar said, tired of being furious. "How much damage can three little shrimps like that do, anyway?"

Plenty.

First the Rabbids grabbed toilet plungers to stick on their heads like hats and on their butts like tails. They each carried one or two plungers, swinging them around like swords, laughing with joy. "BWAH HA HA HA HA!"

They bopped their plungers into the knobs and buttons that controlled the factory's assembly lines and conveyor belts. Everything came to a standstill.

"WHAT IS GOING ON?!" the factory foreman bellowed. Then he spotted the three Rabbids whacking everything in sight with their toilet plungers. "HEY!" he shouted. "WHAT ARE YOU DOING? CUT IT OUT!"

The foreman ran after the Rabbids, followed by a bunch of employees who were trying to get in good with him. Other employees saw this as an excellent opportunity to take an unscheduled break.

But it wasn't easy catching the Rabbids. They used the toilet plungers like suction cups to climb walls. *Thwop, thwop, thwop!* They stuck toilet plungers to the floor, pulled back the handles (*Thhhwump!*), and launched themselves through the air. "BWHEEEE!" The Rabbids were having a wonderful time!

"BWAH HA HA HA HA!"

This was a situation that definitely called for the Rabbids' arch nemesis, Agent Glyker. But where was he?

CHAPTER 2:
Winners

In a nice office on the other side of town Agent Glyker was meeting with the enthusiastic people who ran the Reality TV Awards Association.

Normally, Agent Glyker would be out trying to catch Rabbids as an employee of the Secret Government Agency for the Investigation of Intruders-Rabbid Division. But he'd been put on probation by his Uncle Jim, better known as Director Stern, head of the SGAII-RD, for

accidentally unleashing a giant baby on the city. So Glyker'd gone rogue, chasing the Rabbids on his own. And he'd had to pose as the Rabbids' agent in order to follow them while they unknowingly competed on a TV show called *The Astonishing Trek*.

It was complicated.

The producer of the Reality TV Awards Association handed Glyker a bottle of water. Then he smiled. "I've got terrific news for you! Based on the Rabbids' highly rated, crowd-pleasing victory on *The Astonishing Trek*," he said, pointing to the show's ratings chart, "they've won a Realie!"

"Realie?"

"Yes, really!"

"I mean," Agent Glyker clarified, "what's a 'Realie'?"

"A Reality TV Award!"

"Oh," Glyker said, nodding. "Which Realie have they won?"

The producer smiled even bigger. "The Rabbids have won this year's Best Non-Human Contestants To Win A Competitive Travel Show award!"

"How many non-human contestants *were* there on competitive travel shows this year?" Glyker asked, puzzled.

The producer thought about it. "Well, there was a pretty popular mouse on *Back Alley Adventures*," he said. "But the point is, we want the Rabbids at this year's awards ceremony. The people want to see the Rabbids on the red carpet! As the Rabbids' agent, you'll make sure the Rabbids make it to the ceremony. We've heard they can be a bit, uh, unpredictable."

Agent Glyker shifted uncomfortably in his chair. "I don't know. Where does this awards ceremony take place?"

"That's the best part," the producer said, opening his arms wide. "Hollywood!"

Hollywood?! Glyker thought. *How would I ever get the Rabbids all the way to Hollywood?* "I really don't think I can—"

"Naturally, the Reality TV Awards Association will cover all expenses, including your fee as the Rabbids' agent," the producer interrupted.

Fee?! Glyker thought. *That changes everything!*
While he was on probation from the SGAII-RD,
Glyker wasn't making any money, so his bills were
piling up. He could definitely use a fee. *Besides,* he
thought, *maybe at the end of the awards ceremony I
can catch one of the Rabbids and get off probation!*
He'd thought about asking his mom to make her
little brother, Director Stern, give him his job back,
but Glyker was much too proud to do that.

Agent Glyker stood up and shook hands with the producer. "Don't worry," he said. "The Rabbids will be at that awards ceremony in Hollywood. I'll make sure of it."

Now all he had to do was find the Rabbids. . . .

CHAPTER 3:

Factory Fun

Back at the toilet plunger factory the Rabbids had created complete toilet plunger chaos and mayhem: Toilet plungers were rolling across the floor, flying through the air, and bouncing off the walls! Whenever the factory employees tried to catch the Rabbids, they ended up getting smacked in the face with their own toilet plungers. *THHHWACK!*

"You know," one employee said, rubbing his

face, "I'm starting to think we make these plung-ers a little *too* sturdy and reliable!"

The factory foreman saw that they were getting nowhere. He grabbed his phone and called the Secret Government Agency for the Investigation of Intruders-Rabbid Division. "HELP!" he yelled into his phone.

Director Stern took the call himself, mostly because he was the only one in the office. Everyone else in the SGAII-RD had called in sick or been put on probation or been fired or quit. "Where?" he asked the desperate foreman. "The toilet plunger factory? I'll be right there!"

Stern hung up and headed out to his car, grumbling. "I'm the *director*! I shouldn't have to run around chasing these stupid Rabbids! Fine. If no one else can catch a Rabbid, I'll just have to show everyone how it's done!" He climbed into his big sleek car and slammed the door.

As he drove away from SGAII-RD headquarters, he didn't notice the crummy, beat-up little car following him. . . .

Back at the factory one of the Rabbids spotted something. High above the factory floor the factory owner had an office with a big glass wall so he could watch what went on in the whole factory from his desk. When he'd seen the catastrophe the Rabbids were causing, he'd run down out of his office and joined in the chase.

Through the glass wall of the office the Rabbid saw a very special toilet plunger. It was green! It had silver stars on it! It was *shiny*!

"Bwhoooo . . ." he said out loud.

Actually, the green plunger wasn't a real plunger. It was a special award the factory had received for making the world's greatest toilet plungers.

But the Rabbid didn't know that. All he knew
was that he *had to have it*! Or as he put it, "BWAH
BWAH BWAH BWOH BWAH!"

When they heard him announce that, the other two Rabbids saw the green toilet plunger with silver stars too. *They* had to have it!

All three Rabbids started making their way up to the factory owner's office. They used ladders and toilet plungers stuck to the walls to climb up toward the glass wall. *Thwock, thwock, thwock!*

"HALT!" shouted Director Stern in his most official-sounding voice. He held his gold badge up so everyone in the factory could see it. "As the director of the Secret Government Agency for the Investigation of Intruders, Rabbid Division, I hereby order you to HALT!"

"Finally," the factory foreman muttered. "Took you long enough."

The Rabbids turned and looked when they heard Stern's authoritative voice ordering them to halt. "Bwah . . . ?"

But they didn't halt. As Stern stomped over toward them, one of the Rabbids carefully aimed a toilet plunger at the director's round, bald head. He threw the plunger and . . .

THHHWOCK! It stuck to the top of Stern's head, covering his eyes so he couldn't see!

"GET THIS THING OFF OF ME!" Director Stern yelled, tugging at the toilet plunger. Unfortunately, his bald head was the *perfect* surface for the plunger to attach to. No matter how hard Stern yanked, it wouldn't come off. He stumbled around, falling into a pile of defective plungers. The handle on his plunger waggled around in the thicket of other wooden handles.

"BWAH HA HA HA HA!" laughed the Rabbids, pointing at the struggling director. Then they resumed climbing up toward the office with the green toilet plunger, racing to see which one of them could get there first.

Agent Glyker, who had followed Stern to the factory in his crummy, beat-up car, smiled as he watched his boss flounder in the pile of toilet plungers. He could do so much better than the director. You wouldn't see *him* with a toilet plunger stuck on his head! This was his chance—all he had to do was somehow get the Rabbids to follow him to Hollywood. Simple!

As he watched the Rabbids climb up toward the owner's office, he spotted what they were heading toward: the green toilet plunger with silver stars. It was shiny, and the Rabbids liked shiny things. And they *loved* toilet plungers! So that must be what they wanted! All Glyker had to do was beat them to it!

Lucky for Glyker, the Rabbids didn't understand elevators.

The agent ran to the elevator, pressed the button, and quickly rode up to the owner's office. He sprinted into the office and grabbed the green toilet plunger.

Through the big glass wall, the Rabbids saw Glyker take the shiny plunger. "BWAAAAH!" they screamed.

Clutching the green plunger tightly, Agent Glyker hurried out of the factory. The Rabbids ran out after him, yelling "BWAH BWAH BWAH BWUH!" They might have meant "AFTER THAT TOILET PLUNGER!" or "WE ARE REALLY MAD!" but no one knew, since no one in the factory spoke Rabbid.

CHAPTER 4:

Stop That Plunger!

The Rabbids ran out of the toilet plunger factory. They stopped and looked around. "Bwah bwah bwah bwhee bwo bwo?" one of them asked. The other two shrugged.

Then one of the Rabbids pointed. "BWAH HA!"

He was pointing at Glyker! The secret agent was standing at the edge of the factory's parking lot, waving the green plunger with the silver stars! "Come and get it!" he yelled. Then he ran down the sidewalk, holding the shining metal plunger high in the air so the Rabbids could see it.

The Rabbids took off after him, running as fast as their short legs could go.

As Glyker sprinted past a house, a big brown dog with long teeth barked at him. *WOOF! WOOF! WOOF! WOOF!* It leaped over the small fence surrounding the house's yard and ran after Glyker, growling and barking.

The Rabbids saw the fierce dog chasing Glyker. They figured the dog wanted the same thing they did: the green toilet plunger with the silver stars! They ran even faster, huffing and puffing, trying to catch up.

One of the Rabbids spotted a large bone in someone's yard and grabbed it. Maybe if he threw it at that running man with the green toilet plunger, he would stop running!

Just as the snarling dog leaped toward Glyker, aiming at biting his butt, the Rabbid threw his bone. It spun through the air. *Whit, whit, whit!* The vicious hound saw the bone and changed course midair.

32

CLOMP! His mighty jaws caught the bone. He landed and settled down to gnaw on the bone, forgetting all about Agent Glyker.

The Rabbids patted the dog on the head as they ran by.

At the top of a long, steep hill one of the Rabbids spotted an old toy wagon by the side of the road. "BWAH BWAH BWAH!" he shouted, motioning to his two fellow invaders. All three jumped in, and they zoomed down the hill after Agent Glyker! "BWAAAAH!"

Glyker looked back and saw the Rabbids rolling straight at him in the wagon. They were gaining on him rapidly! He couldn't let them catch him before he reached the train station! Even though his legs were aching, he forced himself to run up another steep hill.

When the Rabbids reached the bottom of the next hill, their wagon slowed to a stop. The Rabbid who'd found the wagon in the first place wagged his finger at the other two, shouting, "BWAH BWAH BWAH BWUH BWAY BWHOO!"

He seemed to be telling them to get out and push the wagon up the hill after Glyker. He thought of himself as the leader, but the other two didn't. They sat in the wagon with their arms folded, shaking their heads.

"BWAH BWAH BWAH BWUH BWAY BWHOO!" the Rabbid screamed even louder. This time he swung a toilet plunger at the other two.

They jumped out of the wagon and started pushing it up the hill. Satisfied, the leader stood in the wagon, pointing his toilet plunger forward.

Even though they made slow progress this way, the Rabbids managed to keep Glyker in sight. (Because he didn't want to lose them . . . although they didn't seem to realize that.)

But the two Rabbids who were pushing the wagon were getting tired. Fed up, they jumped into the wagon to ride.

Without anyone pushing, the wagon rolled back down the steep hill, gaining speed as it went. "BWAAAAH!" screamed the Rabbids.

When they reach the bottom, they looked up at the top of the hill. Glyker was standing there, waving the green plunger.

One of the Rabbids saw something nearby and got an idea. He ran off, and came back with two fire extinguishers. "BWAH BWAH!" he announced triumphantly.

The Rabbids quickly attached the two fire extinguishers to their wagon. They jumped into the wagon and fired up the extinguishers. *WHOOOOSH!!!* Foam sprayed out of the two extinguishers! The force of the blasts shot the wagon up the hill toward Glyker.

"BWAAAAAH!" screamed the Rabbids as they

reached the peak of the hill and kept right on going, flying into the air and over Glyker's head. They desperately grabbed at the green plunger, trying to snag it, but Glyker snatched it away just in time.

In their extinguisher-powered wagon, the three Rabbids hit the ground—*WHAM!*—and sped out of sight!

CHAPTER 5:

Loco Motion

Agent Glyker ran after the speeding Rabbids, heading in the direction their wagon had gone.

It didn't take long to find them.

The wagon had crashed into a tree. The Rabbids sat on the ground, looking a little dazed. One of them had a bird's nest on its head.

Glyker whistled, waving the green metal plunger with the silver stars. "Hey!" he shouted. "Over here! Naah! Naah! Naah! Can't catch me!"

The Rabbids whipped their heads around, staring at Glyker. They might not have understood human language, but "Naah! Naah! Naah!" meant the same thing all across the galaxy. They leaped to their feet and ran after him.

Agent Glyker led the Rabbids straight to the train station. He jumped onto the train heading west to Hollywood and found the conductor. "Four tickets to Hollywood, please!" he said, a little out of breath.

"*Four* tickets?" the conductor asked, confused.

Glyker nodded. "That's right," he said. "One for me, and three for my . . . friends."

"Where are your friends?" the conductor asked. "We're about to pull out of the station!"

Glyker pointed. "Right there."

The three Rabbids were climbing into the train. When they saw what was inside—seats! windows! bathrooms!—they forgot all about Glyker and the green toilet plunger. At least for the moment.

"BWAH HA!" they cried, delighted by the train. They started running up and down the aisles, jumping on top of seats, and climbing into the luggage racks. The other passengers shooed them away and yelled at them, but the Rabbids didn't mind a bit. They just kept laughing. "BWAH HA HA HA!"

During the long trip to Hollywood, the Rabbids never slowed down. Agent Glyker spied on them, taking notes for his files once he got his job back:

- The Rabbids enjoy being in motion, whether they're riding a train or just running around like lunatics.
- They don't need much sleep.
- They'll put just about anything in their mouths: phones, shoes, umbrellas, soap, their own fists, other people's fists . . .
- They seem to particularly enjoy the bathrooms.
- When they spot a cow through the window, they all stare and say, "Bwhooooooaaaa."
- They're very curious about what people have in their suitcases, purses, hats, and pockets.
- Rabbids are not popular with their fellow passengers.

But Glyker couldn't just spend the whole trip hiding from the Rabbids, observing them and taking notes. He had to make sure they made it all the way to Hollywood without being thrown off the train.

At one point he caught them heading into the engine car, where the engineer drove the train. Glyker grabbed food from the club car and threw it at them to distract them. A food fight ensued, and Glyker had to pay for all the food. This trip was getting expensive. But at least the Rabbids had forgotten about going into the engine car.

Later the Rabbids took everyone's luggage while the passengers were sleeping, opened it up, and made a huge pile of clothes to jump into from the luggage racks. "BWHEE!" they shouted. *Whump! Whump! Whump!*

The conductor came running, but Glyker managed to stop him before he reached the Rabbids.

"May I help you?" Glyker asked.

"JUST WHAT ARE YOUR *FRIENDS* DOING?!"
the conductor asked.

"Well," Glyker said, thinking quickly. "I didn't want to have to tell you this, but we're all secret agents."

"Secret agents?" the conductor asked, his eyes growing wide.

Glyker took out his badge and flashed it quickly at the conductor so the conductor wouldn't notice the little stamp that said "On probation." "Yup. And we're conducting a very important, top secret, confidential investigation. That's why we had to search through everyone's clothes."

"But why did you have to jump into them?!" the conductor asked.

Glyker thought a moment. "Top secret," he said.

He was very glad when the train finally pulled into Union Station in Los Angeles.

CHAPTER 6:
Hooray for Hollywood!

Agent Glyker ran off the train, waving the green plunger with the silver stars so the Rabbids would follow him to Hollywood. And they *started* to. But . . .

Then they heard something very interesting.

Across the street from Union Station, a mariachi band was playing in Olvera Street. When they heard the music, the Rabbids forgot all about the green toilet plunger and started dancing across the street, singing along. "Bwah bwah bwah bwah bwah bwah bwah bwah bwah bwah . . ."

When they got to Olvera Street, the Rabbids quickly spotted the mariachi band. They immediately joined the band, singing along and "borrowing" their instruments. They danced in front of the band, and a crowd gathered to watch the Rabbids. Their dancing mostly consisted of wiggling their butts.

A kid pointed at the Rabbids. "Hey!" she cried. "Those guys are from *The Astonishing Trek*! They're the winners! THEY'RE FAMOUS!!!"

Word spread like wildfire through the historic neighborhood, and *Astonishing Trek* fans flocked to see their favorite contestants. Soon a huge mob had formed around the Rabbids.

"GIVE ME YOUR AUTOGRAPH!" each of the fans screamed. "I LOVE YOU MORE THAN ANYONE ELSE DOES!"

As the crowd of fans pressed in on the Rabbids,
they huddled and spoke to each other. "Bwah
bwah bwah?" "Bwah bwah bwah!" "BWAH!"

Apparently, they had decided it would be fun
to run away from the crowd and hide, because
that's just what they did. They dropped to their
hands and knees, crawled through the fans' legs,
and ran off!

"Hey, where'd they go?" one fan cried.

"They're over there!" another fan shouted, pointing. "GET 'EM!"

The fans ran after the Rabbids, followed by Glyker, who was afraid he wouldn't be able to get the unpredictable Rabbids to the awards ceremony on time. He'd never get his job back. And worst of all, he'd never get his fee!

The Rabbids enjoyed running through the city. They didn't even care that a big crowd of reality TV fans were chasing them. They thought it was fun!

And it was about to get even *more* fun. . . .

The Rabbids came upon a ceremony where a beautiful movie star was putting her hands and feet in wet cement in front of a big movie theater. The Rabbid in front of the trio was the first to spot the woman sticking her hands into something dark and gray and wet. And when she pulled her hands out, they were covered in the gloppy stuff!

Intriguing!

The Rabbid had to try it himself. He ran up to the wet cement and acted like he was a movie star, smiling a huge smile and blowing kisses. Then he got down on his knees and stuck his hands in the cement.

The movie star was horrified! Her publicist tried to shoo the Rabbid away, but the Rabbid pulled his hands out of the wet cement and flicked them at the publicist. *Blorp!* Wet cement splattered onto the publicist's face!

Other people tried to chase the Rabbid off, but his two fellow intruders came to his aid. They bumped into the movie star, who fell into the wet cement face-first! *SCHPLORP!* She rose out of the cement, looking like a monster, and screamed. "YAAAAH!"

Startled, the Rabbids ran right through the wet cement and down the sidewalk. As people helped the movie star to her feet, the crowd of reality TV fans ran right through the wet cement too!

The Rabbids saw the onslaught of fans coming after them. One of them got an idea. He stood behind a surfboard being carried along by a surfer and pulled his two fellow Rabbids in with him. They walked along with the unaware surfer, keeping their bodies behind the long surfboard. It looked as though someone with two normal feet and six Rabbid feet was walking along carrying his board.

When they reached the
beach, the surfer ran right
out into the ocean, and
the Rabbids ran with him.
They paddled out into the
water, caught a huge
wave, and rode it
on the surfboard.

CHAPTER 7:
Give Us a Sign

The surfer finally noticed the Rabbids. "Gnarly!" he said. "What are you little dudes doing? Hitchin' a ride? Well, that's cool!"

The surfer and the Rabbids caught wave after wave. The Rabbids stood on the end of the board. They stood on their heads. They stood on the surfer's shoulders. They jumped off the surfboard onto a neighboring surfboard, then jumped back. When it came to surfing, the Rabbids were naturals!

Soon a crowd of beachgoers had gathered to watch the Rabbids ride the waves with the surfer. "Yeah! All right!" they cheered.

But that crowd caught the attention of the original crowd of fans who were searching for the Rabbids (along with Glyker). They ran down to the beach and spotted the surfing Rabbids. A few fans were so determined to get autographs that they dove in the ocean with their pens and pieces of paper, which immediately got way too soggy to use.

When the Rabbids got out of the water, they found the growing group of fans waiting for them. "BWAH!" Then they remembered their game: Run From The Big Crowd! They took off running across the sand with the mob of fans in hot pursuit.

One of the Rabbids looked around and saw one of the other Rabbids standing next to the white wall of the beach's bathrooms. He blended right into the white wall! Well, almost . . .

The Rabbid ran over and turned his fellow visitor from who-knows-where around so no one could see his eyes, ears, or stomach. Then he faced the wall himself. Curious, the third Rabbid did the same.

The crowd of fans ran right past the three Rabbids. It was like they were invisible!

The Rabbids were so excited by the trick they'd pulled that they started cheering. "BWAY! BWAY! BWAY!"

The crowd of fans heard them and ran right back. Agent Glyker, who was buying himself an ice-cream cone (He needed some refreshment after trying to find the Rabbids in this new city!), heard them too and rushed toward the sound of their cheering.

The Rabbids sprinted off, looking for another

white background to blend into. They ran, looking everywhere for something white. . . .

"Bwooooh!" said one of the Rabbids, pointing up.

The other two Rabbids looked up. "Bwoooooh!"
they agreed.

Though they didn't know it, the Rabbids had
spotted the Hollywood sign. To them, it was the

perfect place to hide from the crowd in their game of hide-and-seek!

Grunting and puffing, the Rabbids clambered up the rough hill to the gigantic white letters that spelled "Hollywood." One stood in front of the *H*.

One stood in front of the *Y*. And one stood in front of the *D*. They turned to face the letters . . . and disappeared!

Their hiding strategy worked beautifully! But not for the reason they thought. When the crowd of fans reached the bottom of the steep, rocky hill leading

up to the sign, they turned away instead of making the hot, difficult climb. "Maybe we can still get that movie star's autograph," one of them suggested.

But at the back of the mob, one person didn't turn away. He started climbing.

Agent Glyker was determined to reach the Rabbids and lure them to the awards ceremony. Sweating, he tripped and stumbled several times as he climbed. He was nearly halfway up the steep hill when he heard a strange sound. . . .

Zzzzzt!

What's that sound? he thought. *Some kind of buzzing bug?*

The sound got louder. ZZZZZZZZT!

It seems awfully loud for a bug. Then Glyker saw what was making the sound. . . .

A rattlesnake! "YAAAH!" he screamed, jumping back so fast that he slipped and tumbled all the way back down to the base of the hill.

As he lay there, relieved to have not been bitten by the snake, he heard a voice saying, "All right, stand up."

He looked up and saw a policeman standing over him.

"What's the matter, officer?" he asked as he got to his feet. "Don't worry, the snake didn't bite me."

"You know it's illegal to approach the Hollywood sign," the policeman said.

"No, I don't know that," Agent Glyker admitted. "But I didn't approach it. I just *tried* to approach it."

"Well, as it turns out," the policeman said, getting out his handcuffs, "it's illegal to *try* to approach the Hollywood sign. You're trespassing."

As the policeman snapped the cuffs on Glyker, the Rabbids watched from their perches in front of the giant letters. They pointed and laughed. "BWAH HA HA!" Those handcuff things looked hilarious!

CHAPTER 8:

Working the Red Carpet

As the sun started to go down and day turned to night, the Rabbids saw bright spotlights circling in the sky. "Bwoooo!"

They followed the spotlights to a red carpet. They didn't know it, but it was the red carpet into the Reality TV Awards!

Reality TV stars were all dressed up, walking down the red carpet, waving to fans and answering TV reporters' questions. After watching for a couple of minutes, the Rabbids sashayed onto the carpet themselves, waving to fans and blowing kisses. They had no idea what was going on, but they liked copying people.

A TV reporter stuck her microphone in one of the Rabbids' faces, saying, "Here are the super-popular winners of *The Astonishing Trek!* Is this your first visit to Hollywood?"

The Rabbid stared up at the reporter. Then he stuck the microphone into his mouth and sucked on it.

"Um," the reporter said as she pulled the mic back out of the Rabbid's mouth, "any advice for people who want to be on a reality TV show?"

The Rabbid looked around. He saw a human talking into a stick like the one in front of his face. He started talking, imitating the human, "Bwah bwah bwoh bwhee bwhee bwah bwah bwah!"

Satisfied with himself, the Rabbid nodded and kept walking down the red carpet. The TV reporter turned to her camera. "So, there you have it. Bwah bwah bwoh bwhee bwhee bwah bwah bwah."

Another Rabbid was staring at the sparkly purple dress one of the other award winners was wearing. So sparkly! The long dress trailed behind the lady wearing it, dragging along the carpet. The Rabbid got an idea. . . .

He jumped onto the dress, hitching a ride! The lady took a couple of steps, then realized her dress had gotten much heavier. She turned around and shrieked, "GET OFF MY DRESS!"

The Rabbid jumped off her dress, but then grabbed the part dragging on the carpet. *RRRRRIP!*

The Rabbid took the sparkly purple material and tied it around his waist. Now *he* had a beautiful dress to wear on the red carpet!

"MY DRESS!!!" the lady screamed. "YOU RIPPED MY DRESS!"

An assistant ran up to see what the matter was. She recognized the Rabbids from *The Astonishing Trek*. "Come with me!" she said, quickly ushering them inside. "Nice dress!"

As the Rabbids hurried inside the big theater with the nice assistant, Agent Glyker showed up. He'd managed to talk his way out

of being arrested by showing the police his SGAII-RD badge and explaining that he was on a secret mission to save the world from destruction. The police didn't feel like completing all the paperwork that went with arresting someone who seemed a little crazy, so they let Glyker go.

He saw the Rabbids go inside. "They're here! At the awards ceremony!"

But would they cooperate with the people handing out the awards? Based on his experience with Rabbids, he seriously doubted it.

He had to find a way into that theater. . . .

CHAPTER 9:
The Realies

"Okay," the female assistant said in her friendly voice. "Let's get you three into makeup!" She scooted them into a small room backstage full of makeup.

"Bwhooooaaa . . ." the Rabbids said, amazed by all the stuff they saw. Another award winner was sitting in front of a brightly lit mirror, applying lipstick.

The makeup assistant tried applying makeup

to the Rabbids' faces, but they wouldn't sit still . . .
and they eventually grabbed the powders and lip-
sticks and took over. When they left the little room,
they looked a little bit like abstract art: one Rabbid
had lipstick drawn in lines all over his forehead,
and one Rabbid had used eyeliner to draw circles

all over himself. The third Rabbid managed to give himself a mustache.

The kind assistant led them to their seats in the theater. "You look . . . great. Just sit here until they call you up to get your award. Have fun!"

Almost immediately, the Rabbid with the mustache spotted a table full of shiny awards up on the stage. Those looked fun to play with! The Rabbid climbed down out of his cushy seat and headed for the stage. The other two followed him.

The show's host was saying, "This next Realie goes to . . ." when he saw the Rabbids coming. "What are they doing?" he hissed offstage. The stage manager shrugged. Turning back to the audience, the host tried to make a joke of it. "I guess three of our winners are a little impatient!" The audience laughed.

The Rabbid with the mustache ran straight over to the awards table and grabbed an award. (It was for Best Fight With A Housemate.)

"Hey! Put that DOWN!" the host warned.

"Bwah bwah bwah!" the Rabbid said happily. He threw the award to one of the other Rabbids. The three of them tossed it back and forth as the host ran between them, trying to get it back. To the Rabbids, this was a fun game of keep-away!

"BWAH HA HA HA!"

Finally the host managed to leap up and grab the award. "HA! GOT IT!"

The Rabbids just ran over to the table and grabbed three more awards. People who worked on the show came out onstage to catch the Rabbids and retrieve the awards.

But as Glyker knew, Rabbids weren't that easy to catch.

The agent had managed to slip into the theater through a back door off a dark alley. He saw the show employees chasing the Rabbids around the stage as the audience laughed and applauded. Now *this* was reality!

"Let me talk to them!" Glyker shouted. "I'm their agent!"

He joined the chase as the three Rabbids, thinking they were playing a fun game, ran across the stage, down into the orchestra

pit, back up into the audience, and on up into the balcony.

"BWAH HA HA HA!"

Finally, Glyker and the host managed to corner the Rabbids back on the stage, trapping them on a piece of elaborate scenery. "Come on," Glyker pleaded, stretching his hands toward the Rabbids, "hand the awards over. And then they'll give you your very own awards . . ."

"NO, WE WON'T!" shouted the furious head of the Reality TV Awards Association as he stomped up to the Rabbids. "You're ruining the show! I'm taking away your award for the Best Non-Human Contestants To Win A Competitive Travel Show!"

"But *someone* has to win," the host objected. "You can't have an awards show without winners!"

"FINE!" yelled the head of the association. "The award for Best Non-Human Contestant To Win A Competitive Travel Show goes to . . . the mouse from *Back Alley Adventures*!"

In the audience, a mouse squeaked loudly. He ran up onstage to receive his award.

But just then the Rabbids leaped from the elaborate piece of scenery right onto the table holding all the awards, knocking them all to the stage! *CRASH!* They picked up awards and threw them in every direction—at the host, and the stage hands, at the orchestra, and at the audience!

Glyker, desperate to control the Rabbids, pulled out his ace in the hole. "Look!" he said. "Look what I have!"

He was holding out the green toilet plunger

with the silver stars. It shone in the bright stage lights.

"Bwoooo," all three Rabbids said, walking slowly toward Glyker as if they were hypnotized by the beauty of the toilet plunger.

"What is that?" the host whispered to the head of the association. "That's not one of *our* awards, is it? It looks like a toilet plunger!"

The Rabbid with the mustache was within a foot of Glyker. Glyker smiled. "Go ahead. Take it."

Suddenly the Rabbid jumped forward, grabbed the toilet plunger . . . and stuck it on Glyker's head, pulling it down over his eyes!

"HEY!" Glyker yelled, tugging at the plunger's handle. "GET THIS THING OFF ME!"

"BWAH HA HA HA HA!"

By the time the plunger was off Glyker's head (it took the host and three big stagehands to pull it off), the Rabbids were nowhere to be seen.

CHAPTER 10:
The One Person You Can Always Count On

The next day Agent Glyker went to the Reality TV Awards Association to collect his fee. He'd looked everywhere, but the Rabbids were gone. They must have summoned their ship, the strange yellow one that looked like a flying submarine with a Rabbid's face on the front.

"So," he said to the head of the association, "about that fee . . ."

"What about it?!" the man snapped, still livid

because the Rabbids had ruined his show. "We owe you nothing! You didn't control your clients at all! *You're* the one who should be paying *us* for all the damage they did!"

"They're not my clients!" Agent Glyker shouted.

"Oh?" the man said. "Then you're *definitely* not getting a fee!"

As he left the office, Glyker thought about how broke he was. He really needed to get off probation and get back to work at the SGAII-RD. But his uncle, Director Stern, was still mad at him, as far as he knew.

This called for desperate measures. There was really only one thing to do. Agent Glyker sighed. Then he took out his cell phone and reluctantly made a call.

"Mom?"

Glyker's To-Do List:

1. Figure out a way to get back home from Hollywood that doesn't cost a lot of money. Is hitchhiking still a thing?

2. Invest in some self-tanner. People in California look so sun kissed!

3. Bring in fresh-baked cookies for first day back at work.

4. Learn how to bake cookies.

5. Maybe ask Mom to bake the cookies instead. But definitely pretend that I made them.